GLENMORE VALLEY

Colm's Lambs

Anna McQuinn

Illustrated by Paul Young

The voice of Ireland's farming industry
www.farmersjournal.ie

IRISH FARMERS JOURNAL

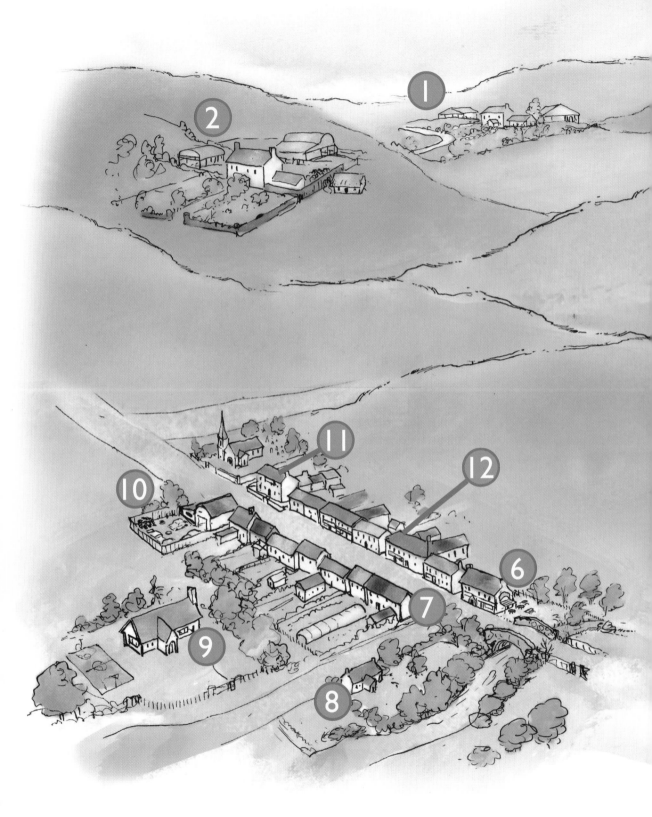

THE FARMS 🦆

1 O'SULLIVANS' BEEF FARM

2 REIDYS' DAIRY FARM

3 FITZGERALDS' STUD FARM

4 O'CONNORS' SHEEP FARM

5 LISTONS' SHEEP FARM

THE VILLAGE 🐓

6 THE ICE-CREAM PARLOUR

7 CAFFREYS' CAFÉ

8 VET GERALDINE BROSNAN'S HOUSE

9 NAOMH BRID NATIONAL SCHOOL

10 CLIFFORDS' GARAGE

11 O'SHEAS' B&B

12 FARM-RELIEF MAN ANTHONY COLLINS'S HOUSE

First published 2013 by The O'Brien Press Ltd
12 Terenure Road East, Rathgar,
Dublin 6, Ireland,
Tel: +353 1 4923333; Fax: +353 1 4922777
E-mail: books@obrien.ie.
Website: www.obrien.ie
Published in association with the Irish Farmers Journal

ISBN: 978-1-84717-339-3

1 2 3 4 5 6 7 8
13 14 15 16 17 18

Printed by EDELVIVES, Spain
The paper in this book is produced using pulp from
managed forests

THE PEOPLE

CIARAN AND NIAMH REIDY live on a dairy farm. Ciaran is 7. His best friend is Seán Clifford. Niamh is 9. Her best friend is Lisa O'Sullivan. Their mum also runs holiday cottages on the farm so there's always lots to do, and Ciaran and Niamh have to help out.

MEGAN, HANNAH AND CARMEL MAHER are cousins of Ciaran and Niamh. They run an ice-cream parlour in the village selling ice-cream they make themselves (along with yoghurt).

LISA AND JOE O'SULLIVAN live on a beef farm. Their dad raises prize-winning cattle and he is also a teacher in Glenmore National School. Lisa is 9 and is very good at knitting. Joe is only 3.

SEÁN AND TOMÁS CLIFFORD are twins, aged 8. Their dad is a local tradesman. Everyone loves to go to play at their house because their garage is so full of great stuff for making forts or houses, and their older brother is cool. They like to go to their friends' houses, but they are always getting into trouble.

MOLLY AND DAISY CAFFREY moved to the village from Dublin. Their family runs Nourish, a café in the village. Molly is 7 and Daisy is 4. They love art and making things.

COLM AND MICHAEL O'CONNOR live on a sheep farm. Colm is 8 and is great at football. He plays on the local Glenmore Ramblers team. He wants to be a farmer and own horses when he is grown up. Michael is 7 and is into dinosaurs, and goes nowhere without his dinosaur, Screechy.

ANTHONY COLLINS is the Farm Relief man and **GERALDINE BROSNAN** is the vet. She is a regular visitor to the farms and has three dogs called Ratty, Scruffy and Scratchy.

Hi!

My name is Colm O'Connor.

I live on a sheep farm with my brother, Michael,

and my mam and dad.

I am eight and I love playing football –

I'm on the Glenmore Under-9 team.

When I grow up I want to have a farm like my dad

but I'd like some horses as well as sheep.

Michael is seven. He is totally into dinosaurs and

takes his dinosaur, Screechy, everywhere.

Even though he's only seven, he's a wizard at computers.

Spring is a very busy time on our farm

because that's when all the new lambs are born.

Mostly the mother sheep – they're called ewes –

are able to have the lambs by themselves,

but my dad has to keep an eye on them all the time

and help out if they get into trouble.

This story is about our new spring lambs.

It was the first morning of the Easter holidays. It was only half-past seven, but Colm was already up. Spring was lambing time on the farm and Colm didn't want to miss a moment. His mother was in the kitchen having a cup of tea.

'Hi Mam,' he said, but she shushed him. She pointed at his dad who was stretched out on the couch.

'He was up nearly all night,' she whispered. 'There was one born late last night and then twins at five this morning. Another ewe is nearly ready, so I'll wake him in a few minutes.'

Colm couldn't wait to see the new lambs. He gobbled down some cereal. Then he grabbed his bike and cycled across the yard to the field where the new lambs were.

The fields on the farm were filled with ewes and lambs. In some fields were ewes that were nearly ready to have their lambs. In others were ewes with lambs that were a few days old. The ewes munched on the grass. They looked up now and then to check on their lambs.

Some of the lambs lay like little wet tissues on the grass. Others were just finding their legs, and some were already springing about.

It was very noisy! The ewes were bleating to their lambs, and the lambs were answering back.

Colm stood and looked carefully at the newest lambs. Then he headed off to the field where his dad brought the ewes that were just about to have their lambs. There was a big shed in the corner where he could put any lambs that were cold or sick. And it was near the house so Dad could keep an eye on everything.

Colm's bike came to a stop.

'Whoa!' he said, pulling on pretend reins. He liked to imagine his bike was a horse.

Dad was bent over a ewe. He looked up at Colm.

'Morning, Dad!' said Colm.

'How's it going, son?' said Dad.

'Okay. How's it going here?' asked Colm.

'Bit of a struggle, Col,' said Dad. 'The lamb had one foot caught. I've just got it free now… There we go!'

Dad pulled the lamb by its two legs and it slid onto the ground. He leaned over and wiped the lamb's nose. But it wasn't breathing yet. Then he lifted the lamb up and put it by its mother's head.

'Come on, girl,' he said to the ewe.

She leaned forward and started licking her lamb.

'Brilliant, Dad!' said Colm. 'You did it!'

After that, Colm and Michael played football. Colm was on the Glenmore Under-9 team. They had a match on Sunday. He hoped Dad would be able to make it. He knew Dad would like to. But you never knew when the lambs would come. Colm decided to check on what was happening in the near field.

Dad didn't look up as Colm came over.

'What's up, Dad?' asked Colm.

'Bit of a tough one here,' said Dad. 'I don't think this lamb is going to make it.' With that, a small lamb slid onto the grass. Dad wiped its mouth and nose, but it just lay there. It didn't move and it didn't take a breath.

'Will I try with the grass, Dad?' asked Colm, his voice catching in his throat. He picked up a blade of grass and tickled the lamb's nose. Nothing.

'I don't think that will work this time, son,' said Dad.

'But we have to try something,' said Colm. 'What about a swing? It might just do the trick.'

Dad picked up the lamb by the back legs and swung it gently from side to side. Then he put it back on the grass. They both watched. Still nothing.

'I'm afraid...' Dad started to say–

'I'll go check on the little one born this morning, so,' said Colm. He didn't want to hear what Dad was saying.

Dad put an arm around Colm's shoulders. 'You okay, there, son?'

'Yep,' said Colm. 'But I think I'll go and ride my bike for a bit.'

'You do that. Can you ask Mam to put on the kettle?'

'No problem,' said Colm, and he headed away.

'Can you make tea for Dad?' he shouted in the door to his mother. Then he took off.

'Ride like the wind!' Colm shouted and rode down the road until his legs felt like jelly. He wobbled to a stop by the bridge and threw some sticks in. He watched them float out the other side. After a while their sheepdog, Roxy, ran up.

'Hey, girl!' Colm said, patting her.

They sat together looking into the river for a while. Then Colm jumped up and shouted, 'Race you home!'

'Cup of hot chocolate, Colm?' asked Mam as he walked into the kitchen.

Colm nodded and sipped at it. He felt better.

'Dad told me all about the lamb…' she said.

'Yep,' said Colm. There wasn't very much else he could say.

Later in the afternoon Colm and Dad did another check of the near field. They leaned against the gate and looked around. They were trying to spot the sheep who were about to have their lambs. These sheep always behaved a little differently. Colm and Dad knew the signs to look out for.

'Only fourteen to go, son,' said Dad.

He pointed at one who was standing by herself in a corner. 'I think she's about ready,' he said. 'And that one,' he added, pointing at a sheep that was pawing the ground.

'And maybe that one,' said Colm. 'She's fidgeting around a lot.'

'Well spotted. We'll make a farmer of you yet,' Dad said. 'They'll probably have their lambs soon.'

Then Colm and Dad headed back to the house for their tea.

After tea, Michael was straight onto the computer.

'This is a wizard site.' He showed Colm a dinosaur site. 'You can go on a dig and find bones and put them together.'

'Shove up there, boys,' said Dad, putting down his *Farmers Journal*. 'I want to check tomorrow's weather.'

'Can you wait one minute, Daddy? I'm nearly finished this Apatosaurus,' begged Michael.

'A Pat saw us?' smiled Dad. 'Where did he see us, this Pat fella?'

'Don't kid around, Daddy, come *on*! You know it's a dinosaur!' said Michael.

'Is it an Irish dinosaur?' asked Dad. 'Is that why he's called Pat?'

'Oh Daddy, now you made me make a mistake…' But just then the computer went 'ping'. Then a voice said, 'Well done.'

'Okay,' said Michael, 'you can go on now.'

The weather forecast was mild with sunny spells –
perfect for lambs.

'Oh, that reminds me,' said Mam. 'Molly and Daisy
Caffrey have never seen new lambs. Is it okay with you
if I invite them over tomorrow?'

'They're from Dublin,' explained Colm.

'Fine by me,' said Dad. He stretched his arms and
yawned. 'I'm going to do another check,' he said.
'Bed for you two.'

'But it's the holidays!' moaned the two boys.

'No arguing,' said Mam. 'Your dad is too tired.'

'Yes, boys. You don't know how lucky you are to get a
full night's sleep,' agreed Dad.

Early next morning, a car pulled into the yard. Molly and Daisy tumbled out and ran into the kitchen, followed by their mother, Dervla.

'When can we see the lambs?' shrieked the two girls.

'There's one being born just now. You have to be quiet or you'll put off the sheep,' said Michael.

'We can be quiet,' whispered the girls.

Mam turned to Dervla. 'We lost one yesterday, so we'll wait until this one is safe and sound before going up,' she said quietly.

'You *lost* one?' said Molly.

'Will it come home wagging its tail behind it?' asked Daisy.

'No, it's dead!' said Michael.

'Michael!' said his mother.

'Sorry, girls,' said Mam as the little girls' eyes filled up with tears. 'One lamb born yesterday didn't make it. But there are lots of really cute little ones to see in the middle field. Come on, Michael will show you.'

She turned to Michael. 'Be nice,' she warned. 'They're not used to animals like you are.'

Then Colm ran in. 'The new one is just born.'

They all followed Colm out. There on the grass, next to its mother, was a small, wet lamb.

'Euu!' said Daisy. 'It looks like a rat!'

'It only looks like that when it's just born,' said Colm.

'Look at its tummy going up and down. It's funny!' giggled Molly. 'It's really tiny,' she said.

'It is,' said Dad. 'But in a few days it'll be hopping around. Now, I must clean up in here. Why don't you boys show the girls the other new lambs in the field?'

The four of them stood on the bar of the gate and looked into the field. The lambs were only a few days old, but their wool was dry and fluffy.

'Oh, they're so *cute*!' shrieked Daisy.

'Look at that little one bouncing!' shrieked Molly.

'Why is that one hitting his mother with his head? Does it hurt her?' asked Daisy, her eyes wide.

'That just makes the milk come,' answered Colm.

Daisy pointed to one little lamb lying by itself.

'Why is that one all alone? Is he in the naughty corner?' she asked.

'I don't think so...' said Colm. 'It's one of the twins born yesterday. The mother should be nearby...'

'Why is he shaking?' asked Molly.

'He shouldn't be shaking, should he, Colm?' asked Michael.

'No, he shouldn't. Maybe the mother forgot she had two...' said Colm. 'Let's call Roxy. Sometimes when the mother sheep hears a dog barking, she remembers to protect her baby,' he explained.

Colm whistled. As soon as Roxy started to bark, the ewes and lambs ran to each other. All except for the little lamb who was still lying there.

'Doesn't his mummy love him anymore?' asked Daisy, her eyes filling with tears again.

'Is he going to die?' whispered Molly.

'No,' said Colm. 'Dad will probably give him to the sheep whose lamb died yesterday. I'll go tell him.'

Colm ran to get his dad. He explained what had happened and told him his idea.

'Good thinking, son,' said Dad, patting Colm on the back. Then he went over to the little lamb lying alone on the grass. He lifted it up and walked to the shed, followed by Colm, Michael, Molly and Daisy.

'First things first, let's warm him up,' said Dad. He took an old wool blanket down from the shelf.

'Would you girls like to help?' he asked.

'Oh yes, please,' whispered Molly and Daisy.

'Okay. Put the blanket around him, like this. Then give him a hug. That will warm him up.'

'Not too tight!' he added as Molly squished the tiny lamb in her arms!

The girls took turns and soon the little lamb was warmer and happier.

'Okay, let's try him with the ewe,' said Dad. He brought the lamb over to the ewe whose lamb had died. The ewe sniffed at the lamb, but turned her head away.

'Oh, no!' cried Molly, 'she doesn't love him either. Now he'll die!'

'No one loves this poor, poor lamb,' wailed Daisy.

'It'll be fine,' said Dad, 'it just takes a bit of time. Her own lamb only died yesterday, so she should take to this little fella.'

But still nothing happened.

'He just doesn't smell like her own lamb, so she's not taking to him,' Dad said. Then he smiled. 'There's nothing for it now only perfume!'

'*Perfume?*' said the two girls together.

'It's my secret trick,' said Dad.

'We squirt a little bit on the lamb's tail and a little bit on the sheep's nose. She'll think he's her own lamb!' explained Colm. 'Anything smelly would do.'

Dad took a small bottle from the shelf. 'Would you like to do it?' he asked Molly. 'I'll show you how.'

'Yes, please,' she said. 'Come on, Mrs Sheep,' she whispered, 'this little one needs you!'

At last the ewe gave the lamb a nudge and he started to drink. His little tail started wagging and his tummy started going in and out. They all stood and watched.

'I'm so happy, little lamb,' Molly whispered.

'Good job, Molly,' said Dad. 'Lucky you spotted him, Daisy. You saved him.'

'Did I really?' said Daisy.

'Yes. It was a great team effort!' said Dad, and he winked at Colm. 'Now, I don't know about you lot, but I'm for a cup of tea.'

'My mummy brought a chocolate cake,' said Molly.

'We'd better hurry,' said Colm. 'Mam loves chocolate – she'll have it all eaten!'